Happy Holidays!

HAPPY THANKSGIVING!

By Alex Appleby

Gareth Stevens Publishing

Please visit our website, www.garethstevens.com. For a free color catalog of all our high-quality books, call toll free 1-800-542-2595 or fax 1-877-542-2596.

Library of Congress Cataloging-in-Publication Data

Appleby, Alex.
Happy Thanksgiving! / by Alex Appleby.
p. cm. — (Happy holidays!)
Includes index.
ISBN 978-1-4339-9949-9 (pbk.)
ISBN 978-1-4339-9950-5 (6-pack)
ISBN 978-1-4339-9947-5 (library binding)
1. Thanksgiving Day — Juvenile literature. I. Appleby, Alex. II. Title.
GT4975.A66 2014
394.2649—d23

First Edition

Published in 2014 by
Gareth Stevens Publishing
111 East 14th Street, Suite 349
New York, NY 10003

Editor: Ryan Nagelhout
Designer: Sarah Liddell

Photo credits: Cover, p. 1 Morgan Lane Photography/Shutterstock.com; p. 5 Monkey Business Images/Shutterstock.com; p. 7 Jun Li/Shutterstock.com; p. 9 Lisa Peardon/Digital Vision/Getty Images; p. 11 Karen Grigoryan/Shutterstock.com; pp. 13, 21, 24 (pumpkin pie) MSPhotographic/Shutterstock.com; pp. 15, 24 (turkey) © iStockphoto.com/YinYang; p. 17 mpessaris/Shutterstock.com; p. 19 ElenaGaak/Shutterstock.com; pp. 23, 24 (apple pie) David P. Smith/Shutterstock.com.

Printed in the United States of America

CPSIA compliance information: Batch #CW14GS: For further information contact Gareth Stevens, New York, New York at 1-800-542-2595.

Contents

Thanksgiving is a great holiday!

It takes place in the fall.

It is a day
to give thanks.

We make a big dinner.

There is lots
of good food to eat.

People love
to eat turkey.
A turkey is a big bird.

Some people
eat chicken
on Thanksgiving.

They even eat duck!

People eat lots
of pumpkin pie.

Others like apple pie!

Words to Know

apple pie

pumpkin pie

turkey

Index